Hamza and Khadija

And the lost cat

Written by
Abeda Sultana

One cool and sunny Spring day
Hamza and Khadija went out to play

They put on their shoes
they put on their coats.
They say "Bismillah"
and off they go.

2

As they pranced
and skipped along,
Khadija stopped and gasped
"Hold on".

She heard a muffled crying sound,
Then you wouldn't believe what they found.

4

"Assalamu alaikum"
they both greeted

The cat remained quiet,
still and seated.
Khadija picked the cat up gently
"Lets take him home,
he must be lonely".

6

When they reached home,
they showed their mum
What they had discovered,
what they had found.

Their mum was shocked, she was in dismay.
She said "O no, he must be a stray".

Khadija asked if they could keep him.
Their mum was unsure, she said
"hmm, let's think.."

She explained to them:
"What if someone is looking?
They might have lost him,
they might be searching".

8

She reminded them
of doing the right thing
"Remember Allah is watching,
He is Ar-Raqeeb".

Khadija said
with a sorrowful voice,
"We have to return him,
we have no choice".

9

Their mum sat them down and continued to say:
"Don't be sad, you'll be rewarded one day.
If you give something up for the sake of Allah,
He will give you something better,
for sure in Jannah".

11

They went back to the tree,
where they found the cat.
They put it down, where it first sat.

The cat ran back to Hamza and Khadija.
It leaned up against them,
jumping over and under.

Hamza gathered some leaves
and piled it up.
They sat on the leaves,
with the cat on their lap.

They sat there waiting for someone to come
They looked ahead and all around.
After a while, they decided to go home,
taking the cat with them,
not leaving it all alone.

With a sigh of relief
that no one came.
Khadija said "We could probably keep him
and give him a name!"

Off they went and skipped along
Both happy and joyful, all the way home.

As they were about to step inside,
They saw a little girl walking by.

She was holding a leaflet
and looked so sad.
She looked so worried
and so did her dad.

Hamza went and asked if she was okay
The girl looked down and walked away.

All of a sudden, the cat meowed
The girl looked up and said
"Mimi, Mimi"! Very loud.

Mimi jumped and ran to the girl
She was so happy,
she felt on top of the world.
She embraced Mimi and held him tight
She said
"I missed you, I'll never let you out of my sight"

Hamza and Khadija were glad to see
The girl and the cat together, happily.

The girl said to them "May Allah reward you
We can be friends and play together too"!

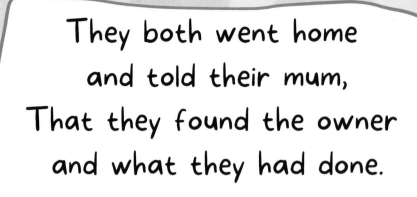

They both went home
and told their mum,
That they found the owner
and what they had done.

Their mum was so happy
and so proud of them
The good they did,
what they had overcome.

23

That night
when they went to bed,
They remembered the words
their mum had said:

"If you give something up
for the sake of Allah
He will give you something better,
for sure in Jannah"

24

The End

"And be patient. Indeed Allah does not discount the reward of the good-doers"
Quran 11:15

Printed in Great Britain
by Amazon

40073100R00016